P9-EMN-882

# The Beginning

## THE CHRONICLES OF
## THE DOOR

## Gene Edwards

Tyndale House
Publishers, Inc.
Wheaton, Illinois

Copyright © 1992 by Gene Edwards
All rights reserved

Cover illustration copyright
© 1992 by Donald L. Kueker

**Library of Congress Cataloging-in-Publication Data**
Edwards, Gene.
  The Beginning : the chronicles of the door / Gene Edwards.
    p.    cm.
  ISBN 0-8423-1084-3
  1. Bible.  O.T.  Genesis—History of Biblical events—Fiction.
I. Title.
PS3555.D924B4      1992
813′.54—dc20                                          92-31116

Printed in the United States of America

97  96
9   8   7   6   5

# DEDICATION

Throughout our thirty-eight years of marriage, Helen has occasionally observed that she was sometimes less than pleased with her name.

Recently, in a somewhat pensive mood, she was wondering aloud if her middle name, Catherine, might have been a better choice. Suddenly she said to me (rather aggressively), "Why didn't you nickname me Kate?" She paused for a moment and then said, "No, I know an even better name!" I asked her if she was serious. She responded that she was.

So it has come to pass that this lady, whom I have known for forty-two years as Helen, has decided to be known by a new name.

With a great deal of pleasure I dedicate the five volumes of THE CHRONICLES OF THE DOOR to my wife

## *Kitty*

# INTRODUCTION

THANK YOU for meeting me here at the theater entrance.

Tonight the players have prepared for us a story about the Door that separates the two universes that God created. The play is, therefore, an adventure into realms unseen.

It is always a pleasure to have you join me when the players present such a production as this. I consider it an honor to spend this hour with you.

As in the past, we have been given the best seats in the house. In the opening scene, the Lord, who is about to create the heavens, first creates one solitary angel. This very special angel is created before all else so that he may record the entire event of creation.

The usher has beckoned to us. We must take our seats now. And thank you again for joining me on this very special occasion.

# PROLOGUE

"Y OUR NAME shall be Recorder. You will enter into the Book of Records all that from this moment shall transpire. I have brought you into being a moment before your companions that there may be a record even of their creation. I have endowed you with insight that I will give to no other."

"You are my Lord and my Creator," responded Recorder. "You are about to create a vast realm, are you not?"

"I Am."

"The books, there, beside your throne. These are my charge, are they not? In these books I am to record all events."

"You are."

Recorder took the great, golden books into his hands.

"My Lord, one book bears the title the Book of Life. It is already filled with names. I do not understand. Whose names? There is no one here, except you and . . . your servant."

"These are the names of those whom I have

chosen *before* creation. I have not brought them into being. Not yet. But I *have* chosen them."

Recorder's eyes glistened; his spirit brightened.

"There has been no creation until now. Until this very moment you have been the All. But before . . . before you created . . . there has been *activity.*"

"You speak with the insight I have bequeathed to you, Recorder."

"My Lord, you have *seen* the beginning even *before* you have created it, have you not?"

"I have seen the beginning of creation. I have seen its end."

Recorder stood motionless. His very lack of reaction was his way of asking a question. The Lord continued.

"Recorder, I have stood at the beginning and seen the end. I have stood at the end and seen the beginning."

"Your words are beyond the reach of the understanding you have given me."

"I Am . . . beyond all understanding, Recorder."

Sensing what he should do next, Recorder placed the book before him and took his position beside the throne. He paused and looked again at his Lord, knowing his words were not finished.

"I have finished all things."

"You have . . . finished?" replied the astounded angel.

*"Before* I created all things, I *finished* all things."

"Lord, you *know* I do not understand."

"True. Nonetheless, place into the Book of Records what I have said."

Recorder lifted his pen and wrote upon the first page. "Before the Creator of all things created . . . he finished all things."

"Lord . . . I perceive you have yet more to say."

"Place this also within the records. There is a Mystery hidden in me. A Mystery in me, unknown to all . . . hidden in me *before* the creation of the world."

"This, too, I will record," replied the somber angel.

Once more Recorder inscribed the words of his Lord. Suddenly Recorder whirled about—"Lord! There is something else."

The Lord did not respond. Rather, light began pouring out from him like rivers of white fire. Recorder shielded his face. Still the radiance grew. The angel began to falter, terrified that he would be consumed by glory.

The torrents of light spiraled brighter, then turned into a flaming furnace of gold. By some intuitive means, Recorder knew he was to face his Lord full on. Unshielding his eyes, he looked up. The garments of his Lord were flowing about him in liquid waves of golden fire.

Recorder clutched his eyes, hesitated, and looked again.

"No! No!" cried Recorder in horror. "It is not possible!"

"What do you see, Recorder?"

"Lord! On your side . . . a scar. You have been *wounded.*"

"No, Recorder, not wounded. I have been *slain.* Slain before the foundation of the world.

"Inscribe into the chronicles of creation what you have seen and what you have heard. Then seal these pages, that no eye may know what you have written. These words are to remain sealed . . . until . . ."

"Until when, my Lord?"

"Until the fullness of time!

"Now, step back, Recorder, and take your place beside the throne. Record what you see, for I am about to create the eternals . . . *and* your companions!"

# One

The Lord swept his hand across the horizon of nothingness. There burst forth first three, then a thousand thousand beings of blazing light.

All, as one, turned and faced the One who had made them. As they did, they divided into three innumerable bands. From out of the midst of one band rose a terrifying creature with a sword so immense it surely could slice eternity in two.

"I am Michael, the first of the chief princes."

Another creature of like terror rose from among the second group, a mighty trumpet in his hand.

"I am Gabriel; the second host of messengers is my charge."

Out of the third host rose one of indescribable beauty.

"I am Lucifer, the angel of light, the most glorious of all whom you have fashioned." With those words, the Son of the Morning rose above the third host of angels and took his place near the throne of God.

By celestial instincts, archangels and angels alike lifted their voices in one deafening roar.

*Honor to him who was before all things!*

The Lord joined them in a mighty shout, joyful that he had won companionship. Joy joined praise as creation mingled delight with praise at the inauguration of its birth.

At this grand moment Creator chose to reveal his full glory to those who were his creation. As his glory radiated out across the stretches of eternity, the heavenly host encircled him . . . the created greeting the uncreated. Only thrice in all the annals of eternity would it be recorded that such a crescendo of shouts, singing, and praise would be rendered with such abandonment.

> *Our Lord! Before, beyond, above eternity!*
> *Our Lord, our Creator and our God.*

"Go now, and explore your habitat," cried the Lord.

Instantly, spirit-beings scattered out across the immeasurable reaches of the newly created realm that would come to be called *the eternals*.

# CHAPTER
## *Two*

The angels gathered into pairs as they made their way across the heavenlies. As they traversed the domain of the eternals, each angel shared with his companion the revelation bursting forth in his spirit.

"I know who I am. By some instinct I cannot explain, I know my name and my purpose," declared one angel to his new friend.

"As do I!" responded the second.

"I am Exalta!"

"And I am Gloir."

"We were created to serve, you know," observed Exalta, looking down at his mighty arms and hands.

"How wondrous! To serve!" responded Gloir. "And yet, there are none whom we may serve. But he has not finished, you know," he continued. "Our Creator has only begun. Before this day is over, there will be more."

Suddenly Exalta halted; his spirit flared. "I sense something! Yes. Our Lord calls us to return to the throne. He is about to create again!"

"Yes!" cried Gloir. "Quickly—to the throne!"

From the limitless expanses of the eternals, the angels hurled themselves toward the throne and swarmed about their Lord, encircling him in kaleidoscopic light. As they did, their Lord moved toward that one place in the heavenlies where the spiritual realm seemed to have an end.

"Hear me, my companions. Beyond this Boundary lies an unborn abyss of nothingness."

The Lord paused and raised his hand. The angels ceased their encircling flight.

In a voice that thundered out across the abyss, the Creator cried:

*I shall create a second heavenly realm. This space shall be* visible. *So, also, shall it have* measure!

"Visible?" said Exalta, puzzling over the meaningless word.

"Measure?" added Gloir, doing much the same.

"We do not know what this means, do we?" queried Exalta.

"No! But we will in just a moment," replied his companion.

Creator lifted his hands, raised his head, and spoke. "Let there be light."

Suddenly light burst into being and raced across what a moment before had been nothingness.

Ascending from the throat of every angel came a delighted *"Ooooo!"*

"Why, you can *see* it!" whispered Exalta.

The light spread out across a sphere that was vast even by angelic standards. Nonetheless, this realm, unlike the heavenlies, had limits.

"In every direction you can find its ends," observed a bemused Gloir.

Something deep within the angels let them know that this second realm, unlike their realm, was temporal. It was *not* forever. "Visible?" pondered Exalta. "And limited."

"And temporal," added Gloir.

With a furrowed brow, Gloir turned to Exalta. "What does this mean?"

"I do not know," responded an equally baffled Exalta. "It is obvious that the finite and the visible are too great a thing for our infinite spirits to grasp."

# CHAPTER
## *Three*

At the very outset of the second day, the Lord once more called into assembly the heavenly host.

"Come! We shall enter the visible sphere."

With that, the angelic host stepped across the Boundary into the temporal realm.

A glowing trail of living light spiraled down the stairless reaches of space as the Lord led a procession of wide-eyed angels toward the center of the visible creation. Even as this garland of angels made their descent, they could not help but crane their heads backward and forward to note the incredible scene that they themselves had caused as they sped down into the visible world.

Invisible eyes swam in the inexplicable beauty of this sister creation. Glory was everywhere. *Visible* glory!

"He did this all with one word?" muttered an awestruck Gloir to no one in particular.

"Is not the light wonderful?" exclaimed Exalta. "It is a picture! It is a picture of the light that is upon the face of God!"

As they approached the very center of the physical realm, the Lord raised his hand. The living procession of light paused and waited.

"In this place I shall create again. Five days shall I labor here."

The angelic host scattered in all directions to explore this hallowed spot. What they found was a string of dark planets lacing their way, in sequence, across a small expanse. There were eight such planets, yet every eye noted a gap in the sequence. Something had been left out.

Or was it that something had not yet been *inserted?*

"Until this moment I have created but one thing. I have created only the *in*visible heavens and the visible heavens. And now I shall create . . . the earth."

*Earth?* queried the spirit of every angel.

"Here in this place I shall create . . . the favored planet."

Again, with spiritual intuition, the angelic host broke forth in a song that would forever be known as the Song of Creation.

Above the sublime sound of their celestial singing could be heard the voice of the Lord, his words blending perfectly with the angels' exuberant praise.

"Behold, the bright blue ball!"

From the Lord's fingertip fell an exquisite drop of what at first appeared to be deep blue water. But as angels continued to stare at this wondrous thing, they saw that what had fallen from their Lord's finger was a bright and shiny planet.

The angels continued their song, while every eye and spirit agreed: This orb, covered by sparkling blue water, was the most beautiful sphere ever to trek across the visible realm.

# CHAPTER
## *Four*

At the beginning of the third day the Lord declared, "Now I will raise the land from out of the dark blue water." With those words there came forth dry land. Upon the land appeared mountains and hills, rivers and streams, oceans and lakes.

"Now I shall bring forth another life form!" cried the Creator.

*"Ooooo!"* exclaimed the angels in delightful surprise. "Company!"

"I shall create. . . ." The Lord paused, indicating to his companions that he had yet another surprise. "I shall create a form of life that is *visible.*"

*"Ooooo!"* cried the angels again. "Visible life? Is this possible?"

"Never would I have considered such a thing," observed a confused Exalta.

"Nor I," agreed Gloir.

No sooner had the Lord spoken than little green sprouts of *something* began springing up from out of the soil.

Without exception, every angel shot to the surface of the planet, dropped to his knees, and stared at the green turf emerging beneath his hands and feet.

"Is this really a form of life?" asked Exalta as he lifted his head in bewilderment. "It does not . . . well, it does not move!"

"Oh, I don't know," replied Gloir thoughtfully. "It waves back and forth a little."

"You know what I mean," exclaimed an indignant Exalta. "Everything that lives moves around . . . does it not?"

But Gloir was lost in his own thoughts as he stared at this green . . . *something.*

"Does this really need our services?" he wondered.

At that moment, a nearby angel rose to his feet and cried, "Behold!"

The entire host turned and began to cheer. As they cheered, the angels (as angels do) began to shout together.

*The Lord has woven pictures of himself into his creation. Today he has given us a picture of the Tree of Life. Upon the face of the favored planet he has even placed a picture of the glorious tree of heaven!*

"How wonderful!" cried Gloir as he watched a forest of trees break into being.

"Everywhere we look, pictures! Pictures of our realm and pictures of our Lord. Exalta, this is becoming a place filled with marvels."

"Living trees, here in *this* realm!" added Exalta. "So much a reminder of the Tree of Life. Well, not exactly the same, of course. There is nothing quite as vast and alive as the Tree of Life."

# CHAPTER
## *Five*

The Creator of all things labored on into the fourth day.

Once he paused and, more thoughtfully than at any time before, created something that was not alive. He hung a small moon just outside earth's skies.

With that done, Creator placed a massive ball at the very center of the nine tiny planets. He touched it, and the giant ball burst into boiling fire that lit up the world of nine planets.

And at the same instant that the Lord lit the earth's sun, he created the stars also—a hundred billion balls of twinkling light.

The splendor of earth's sun filled the day, while at night earth's moon reflected the glory of the sun.

"More pictures! More pictures of our Lord!" observed a delighted Exalta.

By evening of the fifth day, the favored planet

was teeming with a medley of life. Creatures filled the sea, while winged beings filled the air. The attentive angels sensed the sixth day would surely reveal itself to be the grand finale of creation.

And so it was, for the entire sixth day was given over wholly to creating new forms of life. And each time their Lord created, the angels observed that the form of life he brought forth was a little higher than the one before. Nor was it lost on them that, each time he created, the pictures of himself, which he wove so skillfully into each creature, grew more distinct.

It was midway through the sixth day that the Lord created one that was more like himself than any other living thing. The entire angelic host encircled this tiny creature, singing to it with mingled honor and awe.

"Our Lord has created such a beautiful likeness of himself!"

"Yes—one more complete than all others."

"An almost perfect picture of all his ways, his nature, and his glory," whispered Exalta.

They were speaking, of course, of a little lamb.

# CHAPTER
## *Six*

Late in the afternoon of the sixth day, it became obvious to all that the Lord's work of creation was drawing to an end.

Creator stepped back and observed all he had done. Sharp-eyed angels noticed that for one brief instant (and for the first and only time in eternal history), the Lord appeared slightly fatigued. Should he maintain this pace, they observed, he might even need to rest on the morrow.

"He is about to create the last living creature," Gloir whispered knowingly to Exalta.

"I think I know what it will be," rejoined Exalta.

"What?" asked Gloir a little incredulously.

"Have you noticed that each time he creates a new form of visible life . . . it is higher than the one before? Well, it is only reasonable . . . that he would create . . ."

"Create *what?*" responded an impatient Gloir.

"Earth's final creation will be a . . . well . . . a visible *angel*."

"There is no such thing as a *visible* angel!" retorted Gloir.

"Yes, that is true . . . up until now . . . but—"

The angelic conversation came to an abrupt halt. The Lord was about to speak.

"Now."

The word was spoken with expectation and finality. Every spirit pulsed with excitement, for some great joy so obviously churned deep within the being of their Lord.

*Now to my final act of creation. Beyond this last creature I will never create again. Never! Neither in the heavens nor on earth. The physical—wherein reside space, time, matter, and dimension—comes to its creative close, as does also the realm of the spirituals.*

*At this moment creation lacks but one thing . . .* its Purpose!

Every angel gasped. Here was a thought they had instinctively known yet had never formed into words: *Why did our Lord create? To what end is this creation?*

"Now, for my Purpose."

That word had been uttered in a way angels had never heard before. The *Purpose!* Here was an utterance not to be inquired of but to be *seen.*

The Lord, eyes blazing with fires of uncreated light, turned and faced the heavenly citizenry.

"Be it fully understood. All creation has been brought into being because of this *one,* and this *one* alone!"

Expectation was now electric. Exalta was so anxious to shout praise he thought his spirit would burst.

The Lord moved to the very center of the favored planet's surface. With great deliberation, he stooped down and gently dipped his hands into its moist red soil.

Because Creator employed earth's own clay, the angels immediately understood (or *thought* they understood) that *this* creature would belong solely to the blue-green planet.

With great care the Lord began kneading and sculpting the red clay. With nothing less than the full spectrum of his divine artistry he shaped a most exquisite form.

But every few moments the Lord inexplicably paused, reflected, and then fashioned again. This was a gesture never previously observed. Nor did the angels fully grasp its meaning . . . not at first. But there was something they did understand. Emerging from the clay was the most beautiful creature in all the visible realm.

# CHAPTER
## *Seven*

One of the archangels slipped beside the Lord and inquired, with what appeared to be the greatest of curiosity, "Shall this one be above us?"

"No," replied the Lord, without pausing from his labor. "He shall be created a little lower than the angels. At least . . . *in the beginning*. But such is not to be his *final* state."

"Until then, shall he serve us?" asked the most beautiful of the angels.

"No," replied the Lord. "You shall serve him. This is my nature. The greater shall serve the lesser."

"And this creature, fashioned out of sod and clay . . . shall he be as beautiful as we?" continued the archangel.

"He . . . shall . . . be . . . as . . . He shall be as beautiful as even *an archangel*. Perhaps even more beautiful . . . because . . ."

Every angelic ear strained to hear the next words.

"You see, he shall be fashioned in . . . *my* . . . image."

There was a moment of stunned silence as every eye shifted toward the clay.

"It is true!" cried Exalta, who was often the first to break angelic silence with his exaltations.

First one angel and then another joined in Exalta's acclamation. Praise billowed into a thunderous roar, taxing the very fabric of the universe as it resounded across the galaxies.

"I knew it! I knew it!" exclaimed Gloir. "I knew I was created for *something!* I shall serve the one who has been made in the *image* of my God! How wonderful can wonderful be?"

So it came to pass that, in this moment of revelation, angels realized *why* their Lord had so often paused in his fashioning of this clay. He had been reflecting upon his own being, then sculpting the marks of his own invisible features upon visible clay.

Soon the angels quieted themselves so as not to miss even an instant of the final moments of this unfolding drama.

The Lord rose and wiped the clay from his hands, then stepped back, studied the clay mound, and whispered words too soft for any ear to hear.

"At last, my masterpiece. The chosen one."

Angels hushed all but their breathing. Would he now awaken the creature? And if so, how?

# CHAPTER
## *Eight*

Motionless angels waited for their Lord to reach down and touch the breathless clay and stir it to life. It would then rise and take its place upon the favored planet as earth's highest creation—a being at one with the physical realm.

Or so they supposed.

Instead, the Lord turned his face from the sculpted clay and looked out, first across the vast expanse of space and time, then on past the Boundary! He seemed to be measuring the distance between the clay and the place where the invisible realm commenced.

To the bewilderment of the entire angelic host, the Lord left the visible planet and passed through earth's atmosphere and starry heavens. Shaking themselves loose from their wonder, the angels dashed after him.

The Lord paused exactly midway between the bright blue ball and the Boundary.

Astounded angels watched as their Creator reached out his almighty hands, grasping the favored planet in one and the invisible realm with the other, and began drawing them toward one another. Closer and closer he drew the Boundary toward that little planet called earth.

The visible and the invisible were virtually touching.

*Matter and nonmatter.*
  *The seen and the unseen.*
    *Dimensional and nondimensional.*
      *The physical and the spiritual.*
        *The favored planet and*
          *the other realm*
            *were about to touch.*

The most staggering moment in all the acts of creation was unfolding before the eyes of enraptured angels.

PART

II

# CHAPTER
## *Nine*

With the two realms virtually touching, angels now beheld what, though eyes could see, spirits could not comprehend. The Tree of Life was moving out of heaven toward earth! Accompanying the Tree of Life came the greatest glories and most imponderable riches of the heavenlies.

Somewhere within the deepest being of Recorder's spirit were born these words.

"The scene I now behold I will, in some future eon, behold again in yet greater glory."

But words born in Recorder's spirit were words he dared not record.

"The Tree of Life! Descending out of the heavens toward the earth. What can this mean?" asked a dumbfounded Gloir.

For one indescribable moment, the Tree of Life and the riches of heaven seemed to be suspended between the two realms. In that unforgettable moment, heaven touched the tree on one side and earth touched it upon the other. Then heaven and earth began to overlap. The riches of the heavenlies and the riches of earth had intermingled . . . and suddenly formed a vast garden with the Tree of Life at its center.

The glories of two universes had intertwined and become one!

The garden, where the two realms interfaced, was as vast as a subcontinent. The spiritual and the physical realm now shared common ground in a botanical wonderland of indescribable beauty and riches. Creation could boast of a place that was neither the visible realm nor the invisible realm. The garden was, indeed, both . . . at once.

It was the most electrifying and the most expectant moment in creation.

"A garden," cried Exalta. "A glorious compound of the highest beauty of two realms, forming a place more beautiful than either."

Instantly, the angels dived toward the entrance of the garden. There was but one thought in every spirit: *What must it be like, this garden!*

Certainly, the coming into being of such a place had never crossed their minds! No creature had ever dreamed of the intermingling of physical and spiritual glory! Surely it was a place fit for the very throne of God.

# CHAPTER
## *Ten*

No mortal pen will ever describe, nor angel's tongue declare, what angels' eyes beheld that day as they blazed across the garden seeking to comprehend unblendable realms blended into oneness.

Some portions of the garden were invisible, others visible. Some were both, thereby becoming a greater glory than either.

"Does someone live here?" wondered Exalta.

"It is not our home, for we are spirits; the world of the spiritual is our abode," reasoned Gloir.

"Nor can it be the abode of God, for he, too, is spirit."

"Can this be the intended home of the animal kingdom?"

"Of course not!" was Exalta's emphatic reply. "They are of the soil of earth, and earth is their habitat. Besides, they cannot see the unseen."

"Well, someone lives here. Or *should!* Or *will!* But to match this habitat he would have to be a creature composed of elements of both realms. It is surely the most wondrous place in all creation for *someone* to live. But there is not anyone who fits a place that is both heaven and earth."

"The clay! The lump of clay!" cried Exalta. "Look! Its form lies just outside the garden's entrance. The garden is to be *his* home."

"Could it be?" queried an unsure Gloir.

"No, it is not possible," he continued, managing to sound both certain and uncertain at the same time. "After all, the clay, should he come to life, would be of the earth, and the earth alone. Like the animals, he is made of clay."

"Then there is none that can rightfully claim this place," murmured Exalta sadly.

> *Two realms have touched on this glad day.*
> *Heaven and earth are one.*
> *A dream so glorious*
> *Was dreamed by none.*
> *Can this mystery find its answer*
> *Within the silent clay?*

"Exalta, look! Our Lord has returned to his labors."

Reluctant angels abandoned the garden and encircled their Lord. They watched with fiery eyes as their Lord leaned over the mysterious creature who was made of earth's soil yet who lay so very, very close to the entrance of the garden.

# CHAPTER
## *Eleven*

"The creature who lies at my feet shall be called Red Earth, for he is of this planet, and of this planet he shall be a citizen."

The Lord paused, giving Gloir an instant to whisper to Exalta, "Red Earth will be to this realm what the archangels are to ours. But, see, the garden is not his."

But Gloir had spoken too soon.

"He shall equally be, in every way . . ."

The Lord paused, then whispered softly to the angelic host, "Remain here."

The sea of angels parted as the Lord passed upward through their midst. None accompanied him, but all ached to do so, for their Lord seemed to be moving toward the invisible realm.

This time the Lord plunged past the Boundary and on to the center of the heavenlies—even to the throne! Once there, he threw back his head and drank in the winds of heaven, the very *air* of the celestials. The wind of heaven coursed deep within his bosom, where he locked it in his inmost being. Quickly he descended back to the favored planet.

Once again the Lord knelt beside the sculpted clay. Then, to the amazement of angels, he gently began to blow the wind of the spiritual realm deep into the dusty form. Holy, invisible wind from the universe of unseen worlds made its way into the lifeless nostrils of a lifeless form that belonged to earth.

Dare angels believe that things of heaven and things of earth could become one . . . *inside* a living creature?

The hushed, unstirring host watched as that glowing, pulsating wind softly flowed down into the depths of the beautiful clay. The light of the heavenly wind passed deeper, and deeper still, into the inmost reaches of the clay. Finally, the living wind drew itself together into one tiny space, making its *home* in the *inmost* portions of the clay!

This shimmering breath from other realms began to brighten and intensify. Its light gradually spread throughout the whole interior of Red Earth until, at last, it broke the surface of the naked clay and clothed the man in a robe of light.

*Clay from this realm and the breath of heaven
from the other, behold a creature of two worlds.
He is the only being who is citizen of both realms.*

*Standing before you is one who will move about
between two creations without confines. For him,
there is no boundary. The two realms are but
one. I have made him heir to the riches of the
earth, and I have made him heir to the riches of
heavenly places. Both are his. Part physical, part
spiritual, what you see before you is one like no
other.*

*Behold my masterpiece!*

With those words, the Lord moved away from
the clay to watch and wait.

The clay, now garmented from head to foot by
a soft radiance, stirred. Suddenly, his glowing
head broke loose from the soil. With an air of
regality an angel might envy, the man rose to
his full stature, blinked his black, fiery eyes, and
slowly searched out the scene that lay before
him.

The beautiful creature of red clay and purest
light moved toward the angels with a dignity
not unlike that of his Creator. As he did, he
stretched forth his hands as one greeting old
friends.

In that moment, none of earth or heaven
doubted that Red Earth was the loveliest of all
creation.

"More glorious than I," observed the angel of light.

Nor was there now any question about who would inhabit the garden. The best and highest of the glory of two realms now met . . . in a garden . . . and in one called *man*.

"He can *see* us," choked Exalta.

"He sees the *un*seen!" stammered Gloir.

"He is glorious beyond all telling."

"What awaits us when he turns about and the two most glorious of all beings meet face to face!"

# CHAPTER
## *Twelve*

The angelic host lifted off the earth and slowly, almost reverently, encircled Red Earth. The light of the man was drowned in the light of countless millions of brightly glowing angels. The eyes of the living, lighted clay swam with the beauty of the encompassing throng. They, in turn, wondered that such grandeur and majesty could have been made visible!

The Lord, still watching at a distance, lent evidence to the enormity of this moment only by the blaze of fire within his eyes.

The angels enlarged their circle of streaming light until it encompassed both Adam and their Lord.

In this moment of resplendent glory and dazzling light, man—for the first time—turned to face his Lord. Their eyes, blazing like ten thousand fires, met.

Only man and God fully understood the depth of the meaning of this moment.

It is the nature of all creatures to measure others by themselves; therefore the angels had expected man, like angels, to break out in praise in this moment of unparalleled glory. But this he did not do! Rather, the glory of the light in man burst into torrents of blinding light, surpassed only by the light of the glory of God, both rising to unparalleled heights of brightness.

Angels covered their eyes in the presence of this unprecedented display of God's glory and man's splendor, fearing otherwise to be blinded. But on further consideration, each chose blindness, if blindness be their fate, rather than the possibility of missing this moment of all moments.

"Surely," whispered an awed Michael, "the man will now fall prostrate before the feet of his Creator."

Yet neither God nor man moved. They seemed to be sharing this moment on a plane outside the reach of angels.

"They *understand* one another," whispered Gabriel.

"What do I see upon the face of God?" cried Gloir. "It is sparkling, yet it runs as might a river."

"Like a living, melting diamond," replied Exalta in quiet wonderment.

"Behold," observed Gloir. "It is likewise upon

the face of the man. Whatever it is, it flows down the face of Creator and creature as streams of fire."

In that moment of glory beyond glory, it was the man, barely visible, enrobed in light, who threw out his hands and rushed toward his God. In that same instant the Lord of all creation moved toward the man in like abandonment!

The two met in clashes of glory and whirl-winds of light, embracing in sobs of joy.

It was Recorder who put words, paltry as words may be, to the closing scene of that un-forgettable day.

*Late on, at the close of the sixth day, new words were added to the lexicon of creation. They were words fashioned, in that hour, to remind us of what we have seen but do not comprehend. This day we angels have witnessed* tears. *Tears of joy. And something else. Something we did not know. The love of God!*

# CHAPTER
## *Thirteen*

As the day ended, the Lord of all, as a father might do with his son, walked with Red Earth in the coolness of the day.

Casually the two strolled toward the garden's entrance. As they walked, the Lord shared with Adam those many things he so desired to speak and man so desired to hear.

*Upon the bright blue ball*
*You alone shall rule.*
*Whatever resists,*
*Subdue.*

*Mark my words;*
*Mark them well.*
*The garden is yours forever.*
*Guard it well.*

*Upon your face,*
*And upon no other creature's,*
*Are sketched*
*My character and my features.*

*Walk this planet,*
*Walk it freely.*
*Let all things see*
*What God, if visible, would be.*

*Behold the herb, behold the fruit*
*That falls, unlabored, at your feet.*
*This shall be your food*
*And this your meat.*

*Enjoy, therefore.*
*All herbs and plants,*
*Save one,*
*Are yours to eat.*

*This, and this alone,*
*Shall make you full complete:*
*The Tree of Life,*
*Its fruit for you to eat.*

*Last of all,*
*Be fruitful.*
*Joyously multiply*
*And wisely rule the bright blue ball.*

The angels once more encircled God and man in swarms of light.

With that, the sixth day came to its end. And on the seventh day, the Lord rested from his labors of creation.

# CHAPTER
## *Fourteen*

On the eighth day, Adam sensed from within his spirit what his first tasks as lord of the favored planet would be. He lifted his voice in a mighty command that reverberated from the Euphrates to the middle sea. Hearing the call of their lord, the animals of earth, as one, raced toward earth's ruler.

As each pair passed before him, Adam named the animals, male and female, giving them names they would bear as long as the favored planet would exist.

At that moment the Lord of the lord of earth joined him and inquired, "Is my creation good? Are *all things* good?"

"Yes," replied Adam. "All are good. But there is yet one thing that is not good."

"And what might that be?" responded the Lord with obvious pleasure at the insight Adam had so quickly displayed.

"My God, my Lord, my Creator. *You* know.

"Yes," hastened the Lord. "One thing is needed. It is not good for man to be alone."

In mutual fellowship, the two agreed that Adam, like the animals, should have a mate.

With that, Adam was placed into a deep sleep, his side wounded, and from that open wound was brought forth a soft-glowing bone.

"It is not the sixth day," pondered Recorder as he inscribed this strange event. "Shall God *create* a mate for Red Earth?"

But as the angels gathered about the Lord of heaven and the lord of earth, they observed that a mate for Adam was *not* created. Rather it was *built* out of Adam's own substance. Man's mate was being brought forth from his very molecular structure.

And when the glowing bone from Adam's side was fully formed and had become the mate of earth's lord, the name given her was Eve.

Keenly studying this unique event, Recorder closed the record of the advent of Eve by making a notation of his own in the margins of the Book of Records.

*Eve is but Adam, extended. She, not created, is man's bone and man's flesh. This woman, this part of man . . . this counterpart to man, was hidden inside Adam. None was aware that a woman, man's own bride, was inside the man.*

*Has our Lord shown us something we failed to
see? Adam is the image of God. Is there a mystery
here? Perhaps the Mystery. Is it possible there
is a bride hidden inside of God? Will the side of
God, which I—and I alone—have seen pierced . . .
will his side one day be opened . . . somewhere
out there in some far distant moment in space
and time? Will it then be revealed that—as
Eve was hidden in Adam—so also there is a
counterpart for our Lord hidden within his inmost
being? A mate, for God? A mate formed out of
his uncreated life? This Eve is bone of man's
bone, flesh of his flesh. Our God is spirit. Shall
one come from out of him that is spirit of his
spirit? Is this the Mystery now hidden in our
Lord?*

Adam was now awakened from his sleep and
brought into the presence of a creature more
beautiful than earth's most stunning animal or
heaven's most glorious angel. Like Adam, this
ravishing creature was robed in soft light.

In the presence of such beauty, Adam (like all
men after him) struggled to put into words the
feelings of his soul.

> *Eden's first daughter, this—*
> *All that is beauty, all that is bliss,*
> *Thy tressed locks*
> *With starlight strewn,*
> *Thy body, of living ivory hewn.*

*Thy emerald eyes*
*Flash emerald fire,*
*Make captive my heart,*
*Awake my desire.*

*In thee do perfect grace*
*And perfect charm*
*Perfect blend. The face of God*
*Thy face is kin.*

*Thou art that space*
*Where dims the line*
*Of things of earth*
*And things divine.*

Neither earth nor heaven has ever beheld more rapturous a sight than that moment of highest innocence and ecstasy when man and woman embraced, loved, and became one.

The ever somber yet ever insightful Recorder could only wonder things that no other mind nor spirit might: "How is it that man, in the image of God, could become one with another? Is there hidden here the purpose of *the* Purpose?"

# CHAPTER
## *Fifteen*

"Come, Eve, and let us explore our home."

For an instant, Eve looked upward to study the face of her Lord to see if her mate's words met with his agreement. But just as quickly, she discovered that her spirit, like her mate's, knew the will of God.

"Go," said the Lord. "I will join you when you have reached the *center* of the garden . . . and of earth . . . and . . ."

The Lord paused, then added, "And of all things!"

Reverently, earth's first couple walked through the entrance of the garden.

The glistening sun was making its majestic circuit across a sky of deep blue, bugling its beams of light through the palisade of woods and etching the shimmering waters of some far-distant river with scintillating fire. Like a great chandelier swinging from an infinite dome, it spilled its light through branches and leaves, creating ten thousand sparkling lights upon the dew-strewn carpet of grass that lay before them.

As the couple slipped farther into the enchanted realm, the winds of heaven and earth combined their aromatic delights to intoxicate the air with the perfumes of two realms. The sun threw open its golden door to light the citizens of this floral kingdom, revealing their exquisite garments bejeweled by sunbeams and fitted with ornaments of glistening silver.

Earth's lord and lady found themselves immersed in a scene of endless lights, colors, and forms all set against an overhanging canopy of blue. Their senses drowned in beauty so excessive that it reached beyond the measure of their being.

"What imponderable treasures!" whispered Adam. "What perfect artistry!"

"What vistas of loveliness our Lord has given us!" responded the awe-filled voice of Eve.

"Yet farther in," cried a voice from somewhere out before them. Or was it a call coming from within their spirits?

Adam raised his head, looked about, and sensed the air as might a deer.

"Do you hear it?"

"Yes," said Eve.

"A river. A flowing, bubbling river. I sense its vibrance, its splendor."

"Quick!" replied Eve.

Joining hands, they rushed toward the sounds of some distant waters that seemed to be calling them. They had hardly begun their flight when a huge groundroot—obviously belonging to some vast vine—made its appearance. This gigantic root rested on the earth as might a high mountain.

*What kind of tree might this root foretell?* wondered Eve.

Adam pressed his hand against the great plant.

"It vibrates! It beats in perfect meter with my spirit. And . . . with the music of heaven."

"I feel it too. It is as though something within it matches what is inside me."

"When we come to the tree to which this root belongs, I am certain we will have found the highest wonder of the garden," declared Adam.

"This tree . . . it is not native to our planet, you know," observed Eve.

"It is heaven's highest content," agreed Adam.

"Look!" cried Eve. "There in the distance! Branches! And leaves!"

"The sound grows louder. There, in that direction . . . a river!"

As the wind, the young couple traversed the distance between themselves and the mysterious river. The roots and vines of the tree formed themselves into grand archways through which they ran.

"The branches. The leaves. Even they throb with great energy. And from within them shine forth brilliant colors and—"

"The river! I see the river!" cried Eve.

"The river follows the vines."

"Or do the vines follow the river?"

"Or do they flow together?"

As they weaved their way through the great leaves, branches, and vines of a still unseen tree, the river suddenly burst into view.

The couple paused at its shore, enraptured by what met their eyes.

"It's alive," whispered Adam as he knelt beside the river's bank.

"Alive. Water that is . . . *alive!* Clear. Crystal and perfect. Far deeper . . . far, far wider than ever I could have dreamed!"

"Adam . . . in the water . . . look . . . *gold!*"

Adam thrust his hand into the bubbly, singing waters. Turning his face, he called to Eve.

"I have it. In my hand."

With that he drew out a portion of the fiery metal that had been embedded in the river's edge.

"It, too, is alive! Gold that is alive! And there! Look! Stones! All kinds of beautiful stones. And pearl. All in the river. And *all* . . . alive!"

"Living water. Living stones. What manner of river is this?"

Adam stood erect and once more sensed the environs. His spirit reached out to find the answer.

# CHAPTER
## *Sixteen*

"The river has a name. It is the River of Life," declared Adam, with insight from that part of him that belonged to the other realm.

"But from whence does it flow?" queried Eve.

"Its home was once the heavenlies. I believe that even now it flows from out of the heavens. Heaven and earth are joined together as one by this river. And by a tree. Yes! A tree! One we have yet to see. The River of Life. The Tree of Life. They are the food and drink of heaven. And they are here, for *us*. We are to partake of them as our food."

Adam whirled about and raised one hand. Eve knew exactly what was happening. Their God was speaking to the lord of earth from within Adam's spirit.

"What else, Adam?" came the Lord's voice, thundering in silence within man's spirit. "What is it that you know/for I formed you of earth's clay *and* heaven's wind?"

"In this garden is a river. A tree. Gold. Pearl. Costly stones! and me! A man!"

"And more," responded a voice within Adam's being.

"The throne," whispered Adam. "Lord, your throne is there."

"And . . . ?"

"And the man's bride!" cried a delighted Adam.

"And . . . ?"

"I don't know what it is, but I see . . . a city? I cannot fully tell. But I will, Lord, I will!"

"One more element, Adam."

This time Adam turned in a full circle, looking for someone.

"It is you, my Lord! You are also in the garden."

*Within this garden, my spirit sees*
*  A river*
*   A tree*
*    Gold*
*     Pearl*
*      Costly stones*
*       Man*
*        A bride*
*         The throne*
*   and*
*   God!*

"Eve! All this within our home!" cried an exultant Adam.

# CHAPTER
## *Seventeen*

Higher and higher the young couple ascended, always following the river that ran through the midst of the glorious vines of some wondrous tree. And in the distance, calling to them, they heard the roar of what could only be creation's grandest waterfall.

The sun, spewing its rays across the garden, loosed its golden tresses and spilled them upon the spray of the exotic river. A winged seraph moved across the sky like some bright daystar, heralding the coming of man to his rightful home.

"We are approaching a majestic meadow. I can tell. We are near to the center of earth and all creation."

In that moment all the enchantments and treasures of the garden enveloped the young couple and ushered them into a clearing. The aromatic pleasures of the air ascended in delight while grandiloquent trees and floral wonders lavished their beauty upon a living carpet of emerald green. All this now combined together with seraphim, angels, and archangels to surround and greet the couple, welcoming them to their paradisical home.

Man and woman took their place among their visitors while all eyes drowned in the intoxication of this garden of God, this playground of angels, and man's eternal abode.

There, before them all, stood the Tree of Life. Adam and Eve, spellbound, stood before the tree as might ants before earth's highest mountains.

As far as their eyes could see to the east and to the west, torrents of water poured forth out of the tree, forming countless thousands of waterfalls that cascaded down together, blending into one vast cataract that flowed forth to become *the River of Life,* gushing forward to water the entire garden. The tree towered high above the garden, its crown hidden from sight in the distant skies.

At the foot of the tree the living waters mingled with the tree's vines and branches. And upon its branches grew all manner of exotic fruit. Water, vine, branches, and fruit spread out in every direction with perfect union, flooding the garden with beauty and life, providing its food and its drink.

"Eve," whispered Adam.

"Above! Above . . . where our eyes cannot see. There, somewhere above us, above the river and above the tree, I am certain . . . is the *throne of God!* All that we see here flows from the throne of God!"

Adam's spirit began to glow intensely. Man and woman raised their arms in delighted, joyful praise. Spontaneously, angels swarmed about them, adding the crystalline whirlwinds of their kaleidoscopic light to this moment of highest bliss. All things created felt they would surely drown in glory, as man, woman, and angels raised their voices in enraptured praise.

In the midst of the intoxication of this deluge of glory, the Lord appeared, taking his place between Adam and Eve.

"Like you, this garden is two realms joined. Of the trees and herbs, partake for your bodies. Of the river and of the tree, partake for your spirits. And dwell here with me, eternally."

# PART

III

# CHAPTER
## *Eighteen*

Gabriel stumbled back across the Boundary into the heavens while most of his kin, following, fell prostrate upon the sapphire floor. Others dropped their swords and buried their faces in their trembling hands. Yet others stood unblinking—their glazed eyes staring blankly into space.

"The throne! The Son of the Morning sought to take the throne of God!" murmured Gloir.

"Unfathomable!" groaned Exalta, who, at the moment, was bent over in pain, his powerful hand still welded fast around the handle of his sword.

"Had it not been for Michael, we would surely have lost. Strength lay with the Son of the Morning and with his third."

"But *authority* lay with Michael," whispered Gabriel.

Gloir raised his head and looked around. He had just grasped the most hideous of thoughts.

"Will he return . . . I mean . . . is it allowed?"

Michael moved with unsure steps to Gloir's side, his face still reflecting the agony of battle. Placing one hand on Gloir's shoulder, Michael did something that none had ever seen before, nor would ever see again. Michael dropped to one knee!

"If you mean will Satan still have access to the throne, yes. But will he ever again *inhabit* this realm? No! Never again."

"Then, where?" asked an anxious Exalta.

It was Gabriel who responded.

"I am certain I know."

For an instant Exalta thought Gabriel would say no more, as was often his way.

"One third of the visible realm was placed in the charge of the beautiful one. There is where he will make his abode."

"But the favored planet resides within that space!" cried Exalta.

"The bright blue ball!" groaned Gloir. "Would he dare live there?"

"Not *on* the planet. At least not at this moment. The favored planet itself is under the rule of Adam. But the skies above the earth . . . the first heaven! It is there . . . *there* the Son of the Morning *must* live. Satan is an invisible spirit. He is not clay, so the sky above earth is the closest thing to a spiritual habitat he will find in the material realm."

Gabriel paused, then, biting out his words, continued.

"I know that archangel. I know him well. He will not be content to remain confined to the skies above the earth—not for long."

Not quite understanding the enormity of Gabriel's words, Exalta could not help but ask, "Should they face one another in combat, how would man fare against . . . the . . . damned one?"

Exalta stumbled over his last words as he formed them, for he had never before referred to the fallen archangel as the *damned one.*

"Man would not fare well, of that I am sure. A fair battle is highly unlikely. It would not be the way of the angel of light. And, should such a contest arise, you must remember that man was created a little lower than the angels."

Gabriel paused. His next words were hardly audible.

"It would hardly be a contest."

"But the damned one . . ." Gloir shuddered. He, too, found it almost impossible to call one of his kin by such a name. "The damned one . . . he *is* damaged, is he not? And Adam is perfect?"

Gabriel took a deep breath, not sure he dared to share what burned within his spirit.

"I will speak for you, Gabriel," came the solemn voice of Recorder.

Gloir looked up in surprise. Recorder did not

usually speak, and he had never been known to speak for another.

"Perfect, Gloir?" continued Recorder. "Perhaps you might call Adam perfect. As perfect as the Lord can make anything . . . that is, as perfect as anything *created*. But as flawless as man is, he is still lacking something . . . something of the greatest import."

Recorder paused, almost unsure he should speak of such things. Then, with the utmost deliberation, he added, "Adam . . . is . . . not . . . *complete*—not yet."

Exalta had no desire to continue the conversation, but he found himself saying, "That is impossible! The Lord himself said creation is over. If creation is finished, *nothing* can be added to it. If God did not *finish* Adam, he cannot complete him now."

"Adam is as perfect as something *created* can be," repeated Recorder patiently. "But in respect to Adam, something can be *added* to him."

"What?" asked a startled Gloir.

"Something can be added to Adam that is *not* created."

"Uncreated?" exclaimed Exalta. "But there is but One in time or eternity that is *uncreated.*"

Neither Gloir nor Exalta dared utter another word. Their spirits had reached beyond the imponderables!

It was Michael who spoke next, his words uttered as gravely as ever he was heard to speak.

"The winds of the heavens blow within Adam. There, within that God-breathed space . . . it is possible . . . possible for the very life of God to be implanted in man! Of no other being can this be said, but of Adam it can be said. He who is the uncreated *can* dwell *in* Adam."

"Does Adam know?" cried Exalta, rising to his feet.

In an instant every angel under Michael's charge was on his feet. All suddenly realized that another drama, as great as the battle for the throne, was about to take place within the *garden!*

Spontaneously, the entire host of elect angels rushed toward the Boundary.

> *The battle for the heavens is over.*
> *The elect angels have this day won.*
> *But the battle for the bright blue ball,*
> *For man, his planet, his all,*
> *Has just begun.*
> *Shall it be the angel*
> *Brighter than the sun,*
> *Or man,*
> *Innocent, yet incomplete,*
> *Who will rule the favored planet?*
> *Before this day is over,*
> *One of them shall surely weep!*

# CHAPTER
## *Nineteen*

A flash of blue light cut its way through the lower atmosphere of the skies, becoming visible just as it touched down upon the surface of the earth. Whatever this dark brightness might be, it incarnated itself into a tree.

The place of its touchdown? Man's habitat! The garden!

Earth had just received an alien visitor—uninvited, unwanted—who had stolen his way onto the surface of the earth, coming to this planet from another realm . . . a realm from which he had just been exiled.

The root of the alien tree bore hard into the earth. The soil that received the root sizzled, giving off a yellow-black smoke. A hideous stench arose as the tree planted itself into earth's unwelcoming breast. Blasts of icy wind flew from the plant, causing nearby trees to shudder.

The tree was, at once, both dark and foreboding yet hypnotically beautiful.

There could be no doubt, this was the *second* most beautiful tree in the garden, radiating a sorcerous allure that knew no parallel.

Growing upon man's planet were now *two* trees that had come from the unseen realm.

And, like the Tree of Life, there was a life-form also pulsing within the Dark Tree. Coursing through its roots, trunk, branches, leaves, and fruit was a fatal disease, a disease not unlike the brilliant madness of the fallen archangel!

Within the vile poison of this exotic plant lay the tantalizing allurement of all the beauty, gore, and filth of the negation of creation. More dreadful still, the delectable fare within the fruit of this lovely tree contained the seed of creation's darkest potion.

*Absorbing*
   *Ascending*
      *Exalting*
         *Magnetizing*
         *Blinding*
            *Intoxicating*
            *Addicting*
               *Mind-expanding*
               *Damning*
        *KNOWLEDGE!*

Knowledge, in the fruit of this tree, that would course deep into the being of anyone who might partake of it. Knowledge that would cause the poor wretch forever to seek to be good, but never to succeed. Knowledge of madness that covers the truth that its victim does not need to be good, but to have Life!

Another fate, equally vomitable, awaited any soul who partook of the ravishing fruit: the experience of knowing rebellion.

Beyond the skull-spinning joys of the flesh, beyond religious knowledge and the relentless quest for good, beyond rebellion, there lay a fate worse than sin. Waiting for the victim of the fruit of this monstrous, mesmerizing tree was the curse of all curses. He who eats of this tree must one day meet Azell.

*This* is the tree that lies in wait for the lord of earth.

# CHAPTER
## *Twenty*

"Come," said the Lord, "we have much of which to speak, and other parts of the garden to explore."

The young couple bade farewell to the garden's center and its highest glory to resume their odyssey through paradise, this time in the company of their Lord.

There came a moment in their sojourn that the Lord paused before the strangest of trees, one almost as beautiful as the Tree of Life.

The Creator spoke with a simplicity that matched the innocence of the ears that heard his words.

"This is the Tree of the Knowledge of Good and Evil. Of this tree, and this tree alone, you shall not eat. The reason is quite simple. On the day you eat thereof, you shall die.

"Now, let us pass on."

The exploration of the garden continued. Finally, there came a moment when both God and Adam knew that man had grasped the garden's enormity and beauty and that his rulership had begun.

"I must go," said the Lord. "While we have been together, there have been matters in heaven that Michael has tended to. It is appropriate that I return to the realm of the spirituals and the home of elect angels. This is now your home. Do here as you please.

"Because you are my image, you will express me in this land wherever you go. Only one thing do I say to you again: Be careful what you eat. And guard the garden.

"I will return to visit you later in the day."

With that, the Lord turned toward the Boundary, and beyond.

With the keenness of his spirit in full function, Adam perceived that he now stood exactly halfway between the Tree of Life and the Tree of the Knowledge of Good and Evil.

Swiftly and without hesitation, Adam moved toward the Tree of Life. He knew, by the mysterious means in his spirit, that he would fulfill the Purpose of creation when he returned to the center of the garden.

But Adam did not notice that Eve had wandered off.

# CHAPTER
## *Twenty-One*

"Recorder!"

The angel of records laid down his pen. By his doing so, everything in time and eternity came to a halt. The heavenlies, the earth, the stars, the galaxies ceased their motion, frozen in stillness. Nor would they move again until Recorder once more took up his golden pen.

"The page before you is blank. Write what I speak!

### The Record of the Choice

*Man, even now, stands between two great trees. The most momentous decision in all the universe is taking place within the garden.*

*Adam holds the very essence of my being in his hands. Should he eat of the Tree of Life, he will receive within his being* my *being—even divine life. He will become a true son of the living God— spirit of my Spirit, life of my Life. A new species will this day commence. A created being that has*

*uncreated life within him! Sons! Daughters! I will
be their life. I will be their food. They will be my
kin.*

The Lord rose from the throne. Recorder, in
his company, turned to face the Boundary, their
eyes fixed on Adam. What they beheld was a
man who, at that very instant, was plucking the
fruit of the Tree of Life and holding it before
him.

Recorder seized his pen, not so much to record as to plead.

*Eat, Adam! Take the life of the Tree of Life. Fulfill
your destiny. You, a physical being, will take on
the spiritual.*

*Eat, Adam! Your eyes will burn like a blazing
furnace. Your hair shall be as white as wool. Your
feet will shine as brass.*

*Eat, Adam! You shall tread that space between
the visible and invisible worlds, marrying earth
and heaven, time and eternity, as one. The
highest life found in each of those realms shall be
wed in your being.*

As Recorder sought, by his very pen, to will
Adam to take of the fruit of life, the Lord looked
on, betraying nothing of the emotion of this
cataclysmic moment.

Recorder now cried aloud, "Adam, oh Adam,
take the Tree of Life. Fulfill the Purpose of cre-

ation. In the name of that which is holy . . . eat!"

Terrified at the prospect that Adam might not choose his own completion, Recorder whirled about in something akin to panic.

"Lord, if he does not . . . if Adam does not partake of life, if the enemy . . . if the damned one deceives him . . . will you have created in vain?"

The Lord's reply took Recorder by complete surprise.

"Turn the page, Recorder."

Immediately Recorder turned to a page upon which nothing had been penned.

"Write these words, and these alone."

*Whether Adam partakes of my life, or whether he chooses another course, my Purpose will be ful-filled. Never will there occur an event that will prevent the Purpose for which I have formed the worlds.*

"Now, Recorder, seal this page. And as you do, forget what you have written. This page will remain sealed and forgotten even by you . . . until that day of all days . . . when all things will be revealed."

Recorder obeyed, but he also did something he had never done before. He sprinkled the words he had written with angelic tears.

# PART

# IV

# CHAPTER
## *Twenty-Two*

Adam gazed at the beauty of the light that radiated from within the fruit of the Tree of Life. The glow of the fruit met the soft glow of light that covered him. He pressed the fruit hard to his lips. He could now smell the fruit's exotic aroma. Opening his mouth, his whole being sensed that he was becoming one with the fruit. Almost in rapture he began to close his teeth upon the fruit. He could now feel its fiber beginning to tear. In a moment, the very fruit of life itself would be coursing through his being.

At that instant, Adam heard a voice crying out for his attention.

"Red Earth!"

Adam turned to see who had called.

"Red Earth, come see what I have learned!"

Adam laid aside the uneaten fruit and walked toward his mate.

"What is it, Eve, that you have discovered?" asked a cautious Adam.

"It's about the tree. The one that is richer than all other trees in the garden."

Innocently, the unflawed man took his wife's hand and walked with her in the direction from which she had come, not knowing they were spending the last moments of sanity their species would ever know.

Eve suddenly broke away from Adam and began to run, calling as she did. "This way. Quickly, this way!"

When Adam caught sight of her again, Eve was in deep conversation with someone . . . or something.

"Who is this?" wondered Adam aloud.

A few more steps and he saw the lithe, beautiful form of a serpent, its dark body glistening like black fire as it swayed back and forth. The snake was speaking to Eve in an entrancing whisper.

Eve motioned to Adam in innocent excitement.

"Come, Red Earth," said Eve, beckoning her mate to come closer so that he might hear the melodic words of the serpent.

"Listen to what our reptilian friend is saying concerning the Tree of Good."

"Tree of Good?" questioned Adam thoughtfully. "What is the Tree of Good?"

Adam bent lower to hear the whispering of the serpent's voice.

"Has God said . . ." were the words Adam first distinguished.

"Has God said you shall not eat of this tree?" repeated the serpent, apparently mystified at God's strange command.

In that moment, in realms invisible, the entire heavenly host rushed toward the garden's edge. All knew they were not to intrude on this drama, but none could refrain from crying frantically within their spirits:

*ADAM, GUARD THE GARDEN!*
*RED EARTH, GUARD THE GARDEN!*

Adam paused for a moment, turned his head about, blinked his eyes, and then responded.

"Yes, I believe those were his exact words."

"Or even touch it?" queried Serpent.

While he spoke, Serpent continued swaying back and forth, his tongue darting in and out of his mouth.

Not waiting for an answer, Serpent began moving his head about, seeking to discover anyone nearby who might have unbelieving ears.

Lowering his already soft whisper to an almost inaudible hiss, he continued: "The truth is . . ." Serpent stopped.

Adam blinked again and shifted nervously.

Serpent lifted his head once more, scanned

the leafy landscape, dropped his head slightly, and continued in silence.

The spirit in every elect angel froze. Some covered their eyes in dread. Others covered their ears in fear of what they might hear.

"The truth is . . . *what?*" asked an impatient Adam.

A groan of horror and agony rose from the throat of every angel. Some dropped to their knees; others turned their heads; still others rushed back into the invisible realm, there to fall prostrate before the throne. Others, though they knew it was now a situation beyond hope, nonetheless cried out again.

*ADAM, GUARD THE GARDEN!*

A day that had already held one tragedy for the angelic host was about to contain another. Angels began to weep.

The serpent was drawing even closer to Adam, his head rhythmically gliding back and forth. "The truth is that you will not die, rather . . ."

Serpent paused and moved so close to Adam that his serpentine head disappeared in the light of Adam's glow.

"The truth is that you shall be . . ."

Serpent's eyes now flashed with fire, his tongue whipped about rapidly. Finally he whispered, below the reach of any ear except Adam's:

*You shall be as* God.

Adam was fully enthralled at such a revelation. "Could this be why our Lord told me not to . . ." His voice trailed off into rationalizing silence.

# CHAPTER
## *Twenty-three*

A strange sense of both foreboding and grand destiny encroached upon Eve's spirit. She tried to shake off a cold chill, failing to notice that her vestments of light had dimmed for an instant, as had Adam's. Neither did she notice that the entire planet seemed to quiver slightly.

"Eat, then!"

Eve looked about to see who had spoken. Was it the serpent's voice? Or someone else's? Was it from without? Or from within? She could not tell for certain.

"Eat. You shall not die!"

The words reverberated in Adam's head while his mind swirled with intoxicating dreams.

"You shall be as . . . God . . . knowing . . ."

Adam stood transfixed before the forbidden tree. From some distant realm, one lone angel lifted a final plea:

"Adam! Guard the garden!"

At the same moment Eve plucked a piece of the beautiful fruit that now shone iridescent in her hand and slipped the fruit into her mouth. Compelled by some strange inner force, she heard herself say to her mate, "Eat."

She thrust the fruit into Adam's hands. Sounding surprisingly like the serpent, she whispered, "Eat! It is good!"

For an instant Adam hesitated, then, noting that Eve was still very much alive, he opened his mouth and closed his teeth on the forbidden fruit. With hands trembling and eyes blazing, Adam swallowed damnation while his eyes sparkled like black diamonds.

At that moment a deep, rolling rumble, growing to become a thunderous roar, sped across the planet, then out into space and across creation itself.

The favored planet's wholeness shattered into pieces as Adam's teeth broke into the forbidden fruit. Creation had begun its fall from glory in lock step with the fall of Adam.

The heady draught Adam swallowed poured down his throat and into his entire body.

His body! That was where the disease of the tree would make its home.

Adam's body began to change! His eyes glowed like milky fire, his body spasmed, and for the first time his vestment of light blinked.

In his brain Adam seemed to be peering into

some distant, nonexistent realm, drowning in nonexistent truths.

The watching angels screamed as they watched the fall of the lord of earth.

Adam's enfolding light flared wildly as he writhed and swayed as one dancing to some torturous music whose rhythm matched the cadence of a battle raging within his soul.

His body's contortions grew more violent, then suddenly ceased. Adam threw up his hands in what appeared to be a grotesque act of worship. His arms flailed in the air, then thrust straight forward, as if he were trying to throw off some invisible force.

As the disease rushed deeper into Adam's body, invading his soul, the light of his spirit sought desperately to flee the repulsive intrusion.

The light of Adam's body dimmed and blinked once more, blazed bright, dimmed again, and then began to flicker. The intermittent light alternated with rays of brilliant black. Light grew dimmer until the rays of blackness overcame it. The light flared one last time as in a final act of escape.

In that moment Adam's body quivered. He sighed in great relief. The war had ended.

The light in Adam's race went out. Forever.

# CHAPTER
## *Twenty-Four*

A hideous cry of laughter lifted off the planet and echoed across the corridors of time and eternity. Its cursed glee, resounding across the sphere, found its way into every ear in creation. Only an archangel in a fit of fiendish delight could ever conjure up such a diabolical sound.

*I have polluted the heavens with my rebellion. I have taken command of the skies above the favored planet. Today I have enslaved the lord of earth, even magnificent Adam! Creation's loveliest handiwork is now my vassal. This day I claim rulership of the bright blue ball. I lay claim to the land! Never shall heaven's kingdom find place on this perverse and diseased orb. The kingdom of heaven shall never again draw near! Let all know, now and forever, I am the lord of earth!*

Then bellowed the fallen archangel one final taunt.

*Hear me, you who are called Lord of all. I am god of this world. I would rather rule this damned planet than serve you in heaven.*

The words of their foe at last found their way to the ears of Michael and Gabriel.

"He is mad. He lives now only to taunt and to lie. But what is this claim to the favored planet?"

Neither knew. For the answer, both turned toward the recording angel.

Recorder's reply startled them. "It is an illegitimate claim. Nonetheless, only by the coming of a Man who is greater than man can this claim be rescinded."

"But that is impossible, Recorder."

"Perhaps."

"Is there no other way?"

"None . . . unless, of course, the Lord of creation *dissolved* his creation, turning the heavens and the earth back into the nothingness from which they came."

"Will he?"

"It has not been given to me to know. But there is one thing of which I am certain. This is *not* the final chapter in the Book of Records."

# CHAPTER
## *Twenty-Five*

As Adam's plunge continued, so also did creation's. The visible realm slipped into a slow, convulsive seizure. Galaxies swayed. In realms unseen, winged creatures covered their faces in shame at what they had beheld.

The bright blue ball shuddered in its orbit, struggling to keep its appointed course in its trek through space. In the midst of its struggle, the earth began a wild and ruptured spin that wrenched the planet off its axis.

Henceforth until the last of its days the wounded planet would tilt on its side.

As the axis slipped, lands and oceans broke from their appointed places and declared war on one another. Tidal waves higher than mountains swept across the surface of the planet, drowning even eagles in their flight. Giant fissures opened in the bowels of earth, swallowing whole mountain ranges. Earthquakes tossed other such ranges on their sides. The beauty and symmetry of the planet's surface was becoming a landscape of gnarled confusion. Undisciplined seasons came into being, each battling the other, leaving a planet unsure of what nature might hold for it on any given day.

The prodigal planet, speeding in an uncertain orbit, shortened its days and nights, never again to grant man time enough for rest nor time enough to complete the tasks of that day.

Howling, blinding winds flew across barren wastelands covered with ice and snow. Ice caps formed; half the planet became uninhabitable, the other half only barely so. Regions of the bleeding planet fell under the blistering attack of an unshielded sun until it had sucked the last drop of moisture from the soil, leaving behind deserts shrouded in scorching heat.

The favored planet, sensing the tragedy that had befallen it, groaned in shame and lifted up creation's first prayer. It pleaded for forgiveness that it even existed, cried out for redemption or—failing that—annihilation.

Across the surface of the gored planet, the oceans—gone mad—continued to rise into the sky, searching for new boundaries. The land mass shattered into vagabond continents roaming the tempestuous seas in search of a home.

The fury in earth's belly spewed forth molten fire, blotting out the lights of heaven, forming new mountain ranges that, in turn, sought to conquer the oceans.

Upon that small portion of land where life survived, the tragedy of the fall began to monsterize the entire biosphere.

Flowers, shamed in the consternation of their raped beauty, mutilated, fell from their high state and became perverted weeds. Lovely creatures of flight that had filled the earth with the music of their wings became pesky beasts of the air.

The curse soon spread to every plant and flower and tree. The beauty of the favored planet was wrenched downward to match the state of its fallen ruler.

A perfect world, now skewed by the molestation of sin, emerged from the tragic hour as a pitiful and grotesque mutilation of a once-perfect creation.

And in other worlds, galaxies tore from their trackless orbits and plunged into the pits of infinity.

All creation joined earth in an unbroken prayer for redemption or destruction, even as it writhed and convulsed in the knowledge of its fall from glory.

This once-majestic realm, now but a wandering beggar, sped aimlessly across the waste of nothingness, ever crying:

> *Save, O Lord, save!*
> *Return us to our former glory,*
> *Or forever end our pain.*

In the midst of all this damnation, he who had once been ruler of earth, and who was now the author of its fall, stood in the shelter of the garden in stupefied oblivion.

# CHAPTER
## *Twenty-Six*

"What is that!" cried Recorder.

The foundation of the heavens had begun to writhe, as if giving birth to monstrosity. Startled angels, both in duty and in terror, rushed toward the throne. The angels had always assumed that the heavenlies were beyond such shakings. And all knew, and in knowing, feared . . . that not even an archangel—nor the fall of the visible creation—could cause such a shaking to the foundation of the heavenlies.

The quaking increased, then centralized. *Something* in the bowels of creation . . . *no,* something *outside* creation . . . was causing the foundations of heaven to tremble. Some dimension—or nondimension—something heretofore unknown, was about to make itself known . . . *in the very presence of the throne.*

Recorder could think only of the Mystery inside of his God. But *this* was not the Mystery.

The Mystery, though secret, was glory. This was something more sinister than even angels' spirits could grasp.

A fissure began to appear in the sapphire pavement. A strange, foreboding darkness began to spew forth, pouring itself into the throne room. Stark, cold terror gripped every angel. Gloir was seized by a sense of helplessness. He knew, in that spirit-numbing moment, that the perfection, purity, and holiness of heaven was being forever stained.

A dark, rumbling cry rose from the belly of the liquid darkness. There were no words to describe this sick and nauseating sound. Nothing the angels now saw, or smelled, or heard . . . belonged to the continuum of this creation.

The vocabulary of creation was useless to describe the apparition that emerged from inside the inky darkness.

Indescribable revulsion stepped forth from the squalid stench. Before the angels there stood monstrous gore, radiating a kind of black fire. Even the darkness surrounding it could not match its dark features. The thing seemed to be all the putrefaction and hideousness that could ever exist, incarnated into one place.

"The antithesis of God," whispered Recorder.

"It is *not* alive!" cried Exalta.

"What is it, Recorder?" asked a terrified Gabriel.

"The breathing incarnation of all that is opposite to life."

"From where has it come?"

"From the *non*."

"Where is such a place?"

"There is no such place," replied the stern voice of Recorder. "Sin has cracked its captivity and allowed it passage here. We know nothing of this thing, nor its existence, if exist it does."

The angels fell back in disarray. Even Michael's sword hung untouched at his side. The greatest of the archangels knew that even *his* mighty sword was useless for combat with this entity.

The Lord rose from his throne and stepped toward the convulsing dark. There was a cracking flash as the two figures moved toward one another. For one brief instant . . . before light and darkness each established their separate boundaries . . . it seemed that creation had momentarily disappeared.

"Thou art Death," spoke the Lord.

"And thou art Life," sneered the hideous form.

Raising its black, clawlike arms above its head, Death cried, "I have been called forth. I am now . . . *forever!* The opposite of all that you are, I am called forth by my companion, Sin! I will forever and forever roam *your* creation."

"I Am all that you are not. You are all that I Am not," came the Lord's reply.

"Yes!" cried living Death as he fearlessly leaned into the face of him who is Life Eternal.

"I have no predators, not even you," gurgled the fiendish form. "Nor have I any equal."

Then roaring with obscene glee he declared, "I have no enemy. I am *victory*. Nothing can stand against me. I am undefeatable! I conquer all. I am Conquest. None stand before me. My sickle harvests all!"

Death continued leveling his leering taunts at Creator.

"And . . . as you well know . . . I am your equal. My kingdom is as great as yours. My death is as eternal as your life."

Transfixed angels stood frozen in horror at such audacious insolence. Gabriel found himself saying, "Even the cherubim find their match in the terror of the angel of death. Is it perhaps their kin? Or is this an enemy for God alone?"

Death continued in his taunts. "I have come for all this kingdom. And for *all* kingdoms. Visible and invisible. All will one day be found in my still, unliving domain."

Death turned about. His eyes, if eyes they were, surveyed the reaches of the spirituals.

"No! This is not my place. Not now." With that, Death spied the Boundary. "I shall find my ministry within *that* fallen realm. I shall begin there, for I have in that place a cohort. Nothing here can die. Not now. Things within *that* realm can die, and die they will!"

Lust bathed his every word.

Death turned again to face him who is Life.

"But one day I shall require even *you* . . . yes, even you who cannot die."

Death laughed at his own insolent words, then turned and moved toward the Boundary.

"Azell!" cried the Living God.

The startled figure stopped short.

"You know my name?" replied Death, in something akin to wonder.

"You *do* have an enemy. I Am thine enemy. And thou art mine."

"Yes," hissed Death. "And when all else is in my kingdom, then shall I come for thee . . . for thee, my last and *only* enemy. My only opponent worthy of my great nonpowers!"

"Yes," came the Lord's firm reply. "You will come for me. And in that hour, which will surely mark the end of all things, I will await thy coming, for I Am thy final prey, and thou art my final enemy."

Once more Death raised his twisted claws above his head.

*And on that day,*
*The last of all days,*
*Eternal Life shall die!*

From within the black glow, a smile of triumph could be seen upon the face of Death. It was obvious that he had no doubt he would one day triumph in all he had spoken.

Death stepped over the Boundary. His trajectory led him toward . . . the fallen planet.

Having watched Death disappear in the direction of the garden, angelic eyes turned again toward the face of God. But his messengers could discern nothing of his thoughts or intents. Whatever his relationship to Death might be, whatever his intent and purpose toward that thing, his will was a mystery.

But if they could have heard the thoughts of God, they would have heard him say:

*No, Azell,*
*On that day*
*Eternal Death*
*Shall die!*

# CHAPTER
## *Twenty-Seven*

While incorruption dissolved around him and corruption spawned, Adam struggled to free himself from his stupor. In the last, vile fantasy that made its way across the corridors of his mind, Adam thought himself to be God.

At last he awoke. It was his hand—the very hand that had held the forbidden fruit—that told him of the enormity of the tragedy that was himself.

"I have lost the light that clothed me!" Adam screamed. "I am naked!"

Truly, the ruler of earth was the only creature on the planet that had no natural clothing. Earth's former lord stood naked and ashamed before his embarrassed subjects.

Half-crazed, he began to run, plunging into the fallen forest, hoping somehow to outdistance his denuded form. As he ran, a host of psychotic thoughts and images swarmed into his mind and mingled with his imagination,

*Stealing his purity.*
*Poisoning his thoughts.*
*Twisting his motives.*
*Enlarging his intellect.*
*Pulverizing his will.*
*And unbridling his emotions.*

Thoughts—like filthy, gargoyled monsters— dragged their way across his mind, forever calling him to satiate insatiable desires.

*Love fell to lust.*
*Joy fled before pleasure.*
*Need turned to greed.*
*Anger to hate.*
*Strength to power.*
*Humility to pride.*
*Hunger to gluttony.*

Fellowship with God turned to religion. And the intuitions of his spirit were replaced by the clear, precise logic of a fallen, illogical mind.

Then came a final, horrifying realization.

"Not only has the light abandoned me, but now I am going blind. Blind! I am going blind. The invisible realm . . . is fading from my sight. No longer can I clearly see the unseen!"

# CHAPTER
## Twenty-Eight

Adam, once citizen of two realms and lord of one, squatted in a thicket, hoping his Lord would not find him. Eve, waking from her stupor, stumbled after him. Their one and mutual thought was to remain hidden from all eyes—forever.

But Adam knew he would soon hear the voice of his Creator. Nor was it long before the Lord stepped across the Boundary.

"Red Earth!"

There was anguish in the Lord's voice.

"Adam, where are you?"

Again and again the Lord called out his chosen one. Adam covered his ears, even though he knew he would inevitably face a persistent God.

"If only my spirit functioned, it would direct me in what to do . . . as always it has before."

At last, guilt-ridden, Adam responded from out of the brambles.

"Oh, my God, come no closer. I am naked."

A heart-wrenching sob broke from the throat of God.

"Adam, oh Adam, how came you to know that you are naked?"

Adam's heart sank as he heard the cry of God. In remorse of self and in pity for a broken-hearted God, Adam stepped out into the yellow-green light of a fallen sun.

The shaming rays that pierced through the garden's trees revealed that Adam had, from head to toe, ridiculously robed himself in leaves!

Adam struggled to find some words to speak. He shrugged his shoulders in bewilderment, realizing anew that bursts of revelation no longer guided his ways. Now forced to stoop to a lower level of comprehension, Adam drew upon a fallen intellect. In so doing, he revealed to all creation the enormity of his fall, for out of the mouth of Adam flowed the pitiful insanity of something called reason.

Incapable of being honest with himself or comprehending that he could not deceive his Lord, Adam shamed the language of man with his response.

"The woman whom you gave me caused me to eat the forbidden fruit."

The once regal Adam now spoke as a spoiled child. He who, a few hours before, was only slightly lower than angels, now was shown to be only slightly higher than animals. A man enslaved to the diminished capacities of logic was seeking to communicate with his God on the grounds of excuses.

The Lord's only answer to man's reasonings was silence. In that awful moment, Adam learned what every fallen son of Adam one day discovers: he had a condemning conscience, and that conscience could scream quite loudly.

Adam wept.

The Lord raised his eyes and looked toward the heavenlies, signaling the angels.

"Quickly," commanded Michael. "Before he is blind."

Slowly, almost timidly, the angels began to gather around God and man.

Adam looked up, his vision of his unseen friends dim and unsure. The angels, who had often encircled God and man, now walked with them in mutual sadness, moaning a forlorn dirge as they did. Soon God, man, and angels blended their sorrows and sobs, giving birth to a requiem for creation's innocence. But the sad scene ended abruptly when Adam, turning to his God, broke the dirge and made the most surprising of requests.

# CHAPTER
## *Twenty-nine*

"Lord, you must not allow the garden to remain on the earth. It must be banished from this place. Now! And the Tree of Life must return to its former home."

"Do you fully understand why you are making this plea?" came the Lord's reply, pleased that not all of Adam's spiritual senses were inoperative.

"I do," replied Adam, shuddering.

"And what is that?" queried his Lord.

"A damnation can befall me—or Eve or any of my descendants—as unimaginable, unspeakable, as ghastly as Azell himself.

"Were I to partake of the Tree of Life, I would unite a corrupt, *dying* body with eternal life. Please, dear Lord, do not let this happen. Fallen life, in a fallen, dying body, joined to life itself, never able to die! I would be forever dragging about the gore of an ever-dying body. It is unthinkable. Even the pits of hell would pity me.

"Lord, this must never befall me, nor Eve, nor our offspring. So I beg you, remove the garden. Command it to the security of the heavens. Move it far from the wounded planet. Forever, Lord. *Forever.*"

"I will do as you say, my son. The garden and the Tree of Life will I send into the heavenlies. But . . . perhaps not forever."

The Lord gathered Adam and Eve into his arms. "Go now. I cannot remove the garden until you depart."

"Help me, Lord, to find the way back to the entrance. I cannot see. All things spiritual, angels and garden, are vanishing before my eyes."

Walking ever so slowly, the Lord guided them toward the garden's door.

Eve, unsure of what awaited them in the harsh and barren land that lay outside the garden, wept quietly. From time to time she paused and looked back, as if to say farewell to her home.

Just as they came to the garden's entrance, the Lord took one of the most innocent of the creatures of the field and slew it, using its skin to cover Adam and Eve's nakedness.

It was the angel Recorder who expressed the amazement of all the angels when he penned these words upon the pages of the Book of Records: "How strange it is, that God can kill."

# CHAPTER
## *Thirty*

As they stood in the very entranceway of the garden, the trio looked out upon the sullen planet.

"Adam, henceforth you must work the land of this now hostile planet and force it to yield the things you need."

With utmost tenderness, the Lord reached out and gently touched Eve.

"You, dear child, are the picture of a counterpart, my mate, whom I do not have. In the not-too-distant future you will bear a child. The bearing of your son will not be without pain. Such is the inevitable result of the tragedy that has overtaken your species.

"With the greatest of sorrow I must also warn you that one day your bodies will die, just as each of your spirits has died."

"My Lord and my God," responded Adam, "what has happened to us? This strange pain, this ever-present sense of *guilt,* it will forever be passed on to all of our species, will it not?"

Eve burst into tears, falling into Adam's arms as she did.

"All this is my doing," she moaned. "I should never have brought you back to the cursed tree."

Reassuringly, Adam pulled Eve closer to himself.

"You must not speak this way. Not now. Not ever."

Adam's rich voice resonated with compassion. "This error of all errors falls not with you. It is I, the once undisputed lord of earth, who authored this greatest of all catastrophes. The disease, with its power to bring death, is my responsibility, not yours."

"But one day we both must die. We shall be no more. The thought is unbearable," responded Eve. "Beyond death there is nothing. I shall never see you again. And if it is I who goes first into that dark corridor, I will be leaving you here to die alone!"

"No, Eve. Remember, and remember well: We are that creation who has seen the unseen. Our bodies shall die, yes. But somewhere out there in some far distant age, there must be life again. Some portion of our being is immortal. Nor shall death be either our end or our parting."

*If thou art called before me*
*To spheres that are eternal,*
*To take thy place before the throne*
*In that bright realm supernal,*
*Though storms of light*
*Do thee enfold*
*Or God himself be thine abode,*
*This heart of mine yet shall find thee.*
*For love's chained not*
*By matter, space, and time,*
*Nor other fetters of kindred kind.*
*And when I find that glory place*
*Where dwells thy hallowed, sacred*
*Face,*
*There—far better—*
*Shall I love thee.*

Still holding Eve protectively, Adam raised his tear-drenched face and addressed his Creator.

"My Lord and my God, even now, you fade from my sight. Though my body be polluted, the light upon my body gone out and my spirit gasping its last, still, *I have my memory.* And this I know: You are not finished. Somewhere out there, beyond this fitful day, lies hope. Your Purpose for having created me does not end at my grave.

"Lord, what is there in the future that shelters our hope?"

"Your hope lies not in the future, my son, but in eons long past. In ages before the eternals, when there was nothing except I Am . . . when I was the All. There, in my own being, your hope was established."

The Lord turned one last time to Eve.

"A day shall come when one of your kin will bring forth that glad day when hope shall become reality. All your descendants, save one, will be born of the seed of man. But once, *and only once,* there will be born upon this planet one who is born of the *seed of woman.* Outside the disease that lies within the loins of *man* shall a child be born. Born of *woman's* seed."

The Lord paused, his eyes glistening. "The enemy shall bruise his heel."

Upon hearing these words Eve clutched her bosom, as though she, the mother of all, could even in that moment sense the pain that her descendant would know.

In words laced with both triumph and anger, the Lord continued, "But he shall crush the head of your enemy!"

Eve wept tears not far from joy while Adam raised his hand toward heaven in assent.

"Now it is time to go."

God and his two most cherished companions bade one another good-bye. Yet each time they pulled apart, they returned to embrace again and weep again. But once, as Adam sought to force himself away, the garden, his Lord, and realms unseen forever disappeared before his eyes.

Taking Eve by the hand, Adam walked out upon the cursed land. They looked all about, hoping to find some small place upon the surface of the wounded planet where they might make a safe abode.

# CHAPTER
## *Thirty-One*

The Lord turned to face the garden. As he did, he raised his hand.

"Now!"

The garden began to recede from the surface of the earth. The Boundary opened wide to receive back into heaven the Tree of Life. That precious space once called the Garden of Eden lifted into the heavens and disappeared from earth's view. In the place where once it flourished appeared a desert wasteland, void of all life. Where once heaven met earth, there was now but scorched, burned sand, a near duplicate of hell.

When the garden and all its contents had at last found safety in the heavenlies, the Lord reached out to draw the two realms together again so they might touch in one small place.

"The heavens must be cut off from man. The Boundary must be closed. Commerce between the two realms must cease. There will, of course, be rare occasions when I will visit the injured planet. And, perhaps . . . on yet rarer occasions there may be need for man to visit the heavenlies."

With those words, the Lord raised his hand again.

The Boundary disappeared. In its stead there appeared a great Door that could be opened only from heaven's side. Two realms still touched, but a tightly sealed Door separated them so completely that the one would forget the other ever existed.

The Lord turned toward the throne and cried, "Creatures of terror, come!"

From the midst of the impenetrable light that enveloped the throne emerged two creatures of fierce fury. Cherubim, protectors of the throne, made their way to the Door. The Door opened, and the cherubim took their places just outside the heavens, in front of the Door.

"Let none pass through except by my command."

With those words, a whirling, circling sword all covered with fire appeared before the creatures of terror.

Earth's oneness with the heavens had come to an end.

Surveying this sad moment, Recorder made the following entry in the Book of Records.

*Thus ends the union of heaven and earth,*
*Nonetheless, there continue*
*The chronicles of the heavens*
*and*
*The chronicles of earth.*
*So, also, begins*
*The Chronicles of the Door.*

# EPILOGUE

The sons of Adam spread across the face of the earth. Cain, the first child of the first couple, grew up to be a murderer. Other descendants, carrying within them the disease of sin, fared no better. The Lord, therefore, destroyed man's civilization in a deluge of water, saving from its destruction one family only.

One of the surviving sons of that small family turned out to be no better than those who had lived before the flood. Only a brief time passed before the face of the earth was once more populated by the mutated species called *fallen man.*

During those times, the Door between the heavens and earth opened on only the rarest occasions.

But there did come a most memorable day when the Lord, in company with Gabriel and Michael, stood at the passageway between the two realms and commanded the Door to open. The Lord stepped upon the Door's threshold, while Michael and Gabriel waited, and observed.

"A place even farther east than the land of Babylon," said Michael, looking out upon the scene that lay before them.

"There," replied Gabriel, as he pointed toward a man intently involved in the skinning of pigs.

"That is the one to whom the Lord will speak this day. It appears his occupation is raising livestock. I see cows, sheep, goats, and pigs."

*What Purpose lies behind the Lord's desire to speak to this unwashed Gentile?* wondered both archangels.

"Look! One of the man's servants has called him to the noon meal. It seems the man's favorite meat is pork."

"Why would the Lord wish to speak to an uncircumcised heathen?"

At that moment the Lord called out to the man.

"Abram!"

*The Beginning* (1992)
is volume one of
THE CHRONICLES OF THE DOOR.
Other volumes
(with year of publication)
are as follows:
*The Escape* (1993)
*The Birth* (1991)
*The Triumph* (1995)
*The Return* (1996)